For Nicola, Eliza, Jack and Tom
A.M.

For Miles, with love
J.M.

This edition produced 2005 for
READER'S CHOICE BOOKS
50 E. Burlington Ave
Fairfield, Iowa 52556
by LITTLE TIGER PRESS
An imprint of Magi Publications
1 The Coda Centre, 189 Munster Road
London SW6 6AW, UK
www.littletigerpress.com

First published in the United States 1995
by Little Tiger Press

Originally published in Great Britain 1995
by Magi Publications, London

Text copyright © Anne Mangan 1995
Illustrations copyright © Joanne Moss 1995

ISBN 1 84506 120 9

Printed in China
2 4 6 8 10 9 7 5 3 1

Little Teddy Left Behind

Anne Mangan
Pictures by Joanne Moss

Little Tiger Press

Little Teddy woke up and sneezed loudly.
Nobody heard him because there was no one there.
Nicole and Jack had moved to a new house.

"I'm all alone," said Teddy. "They've left me
behind. They never were very good at packing." It
was so dusty that he sneezed again. "Achoo!"

It grew dark, and at last Teddy went
to sleep again.

The next morning the cleaning lady's dog
spotted him and picked him up.

"What do you have there?" asked the lady,
and when she saw how grubby Teddy was, she
grabbed him with her big hands . . .

. . . and popped him into
the washing machine!
"Oh, help!" cried Little Teddy,
but she didn't hear his
tiny squeak.
It was terrible in the
washing machine. Teddy
whirled around and around
until he was quite dizzy. He
growled his very loudest growl,
but nobody came to rescue him.

At last he was spun dry,
and the machine stopped.
Teddy lay there among
all the damp clothes,
wondering what would
happen next.

The cleaning lady opened the machine
door and took him out. "You're not quite
dry yet," she said.

"I am so!" growled Little Teddy, but
she didn't seem to hear. In a moment she'd
pinned him upside down on the clothesline.
"I'd rather be dirty and right side up!"
he cried.

It was a windy day,
and Teddy swung back and
forth on the clothesline. It was
exciting in a way, like flying in space.
All at once the line broke, and Teddy fell down, down, down.
"It's a good thing bears have so much fluff," he thought as he landed
in the grass. Butterflies flew around him and bees buzzed over his head.
Little Teddy liked the bright, cheerful butterflies, but he was afraid
of the bees.

"You scare me," he squeaked, even though they were
too busy to hear him.

Suddenly Teddy felt hot breath in his ear.

"Oh no!" he cried. "It's that dog again!"

The dog seized Little Teddy in his big teeth and pushed through a very prickly hedge into the next garden.

"Oh, my poor fur!" gasped Teddy.

A lady looked up as the dog rushed onto her lawn. "Ugh, you've got a rat in your mouth!" she screamed, throwing her garden glove at them.

"I'm no rat!" growled Teddy.

The dog ran out through
the garden gate into the woods.
"I wish he'd drop me," thought poor Teddy. Finally,
the dog spotted a rabbit and ran off, leaving Teddy behind.
Teddy lay very still, hoping the dog wouldn't come back.
It was quiet in the woods–but not for long. A boy and a girl
came rushing toward him.
"Hey, a little teddy!" cried the boy, picking him up.

"Catch!" he shouted, and poor Teddy
was tossed from one to the other until he felt quite sick.
Jack and Nicole had never played with him like this.

At last the children grew tired of their game, and the
girl flung Little Teddy high into the air.

Up, up, up he sailed, right into the branches of a tall
tree. No sooner had he landed than he heard an angry
chattering noise.

"Trying to steal my nuts, are you?"

Teddy looked down from his perch. On the next branch a squirrel was glaring at him. Teddy tried to explain about the boy and girl and their awful game of catch, but the squirrel didn't seem to hear. "This is my tree!" he said, giving Teddy a sudden push. The little bear fell down, down, down . . .

. . . and landed on a wooden floor.

He was still getting his breath back
and wondering how Jack and Nicole would
ever find him, when he heard children's voices.
He tried his growl and he tried his squeak, but
they were too small for anyone to hear him.

The floor was as dusty as the empty room he
had left behind. Once again Little Teddy began to
sneeze and sneeze. The sneezes were louder than
the growls and squeaks, and soon the voices
came nearer . . .

"Look, there's a ladder!"

"It's a tree house!"

Two faces were peering at him—two faces he knew very well!

"It's Little Teddy!" cried Jack. "How did he get into our new yard? I thought he was still packed up."

"I don't know," said Nicole, giving Teddy a hug. "Maybe he's been exploring his new home. What a wonderful tree house he's found!"

"Let's call it the Teddy House," said Jack.

His very own house! Little Teddy liked the idea.

A few days later, Nicole and Jack had a housewarming party for all their friends. And each friend brought a teddy bear, so that Little Teddy could have his *own* party in his new home in the big tree.